To Lily
Enjoy!
Janice Tesch-Cassady

MW01094877

The Purple Teddy Bear

A Christmas Story

Written and Illustrated by **Janie Tesch-Cassady**

Two Harbors Press
322 First Avenue N, 5th floor
Minneapolis, MN 55401
612.455.2293
www.TwoHarborsPress.com

ISBN-13: 978-1-63413-707-2
LCCN: 2015912225

Distributed by Itasca Books

Cover Design by Sophie Chi
Typeset by Emily Keenan
Illustrations by Janie Tesch-Cassady
The illustrations were rendered in ink and watercolor.

Printed in the United States of America

Many thanks to all my children, grandchildren, and other family for their help getting *The Purple Teddy Bear* published and for providing encouragement.

For Robin, Teri, Paula,
Mary Lee, and Heather
The Awesome Five

On that first Christmas
As prophets had said,
A savior was born
In a manger bed.

Amazing things happened
On that night,
Up in the sky
Was a star so bright.

And angels singing
Their songs of joy,
To celebrate the birth
Of this baby boy.

And now at Christmas
Our voices we raise,
Singing the songs
Of joy and praise.

It was the day before Christmas. Santa's helpers were hurrying about, getting toys wrapped and ready for Santa's big trip.

Santa was going over his list to make sure he had not missed anyone. He was also checking the letters he had received to make sure he was giving all the boys and girls what they wanted.

"At last," he said as he finished reading the last letter, "all through at last!"

Then he noticed something behind his desk in the dark, dusty corner — a letter he had never opened.

He quickly opened the letter and read it aloud:

Dear Santa,

I am four years old. I have been good all year. Please may I have a teddy bear for Christmas? When you come to my house there will be cookies and a glass of milk waiting for you.

Love, Sam

Santa smiled. "He knows I like cookies," he said to himself as he hurried off to tell his helpers about the letter.

Quick as the *swish* of a reindeer's tail, Santa's helpers were busy looking for the right color of fuzzy fabric to make Sam's teddy bear. They looked in every corner, in every box, and on every shelf of the sewing room, but there was no brown, tan, or other teddy bear–colored fabric left. It had all been used for the other teddy bears and toy animals.

The only color of fabric they could find was purple.

Santa's helpers had never made a purple teddy bear
before, but because there was only purple fuzzy
fabric left, and because Sam really wanted a teddy
bear, they made a purple teddy bear just for Sam.

The teddy bear had black button eyes, a little black nose, and a blue ribbon around his neck. When the helpers were all finished, he was just the kind of teddy bear anyone would want to cuddle.

When Santa saw the teddy bear, he laughed until he shook all over. "Ho, ho, ho! You are a cute little fellow," he said. "I will call you Teddy."

Santa took Teddy into a room that was filled with dolls and teddy bears and toy animals of every kind. He set the teddy bear down on a long table with some other toys. There were brown teddy bears and tan teddy bears, but Teddy was the only purple teddy bear.

After Santa left the room, the dolls started to snicker and laugh as they glanced at Teddy.

One doll said, "Who ever saw a purple teddy bear?" Then all of the dolls, teddy bears, and other toy animals began to laugh too. Teddy did not know what was so funny, but he laughed along with them.

Another doll said, "Who would ever want a purple teddy bear?"

This made all the toys laugh even more — except Teddy, who felt very sad. He did not know why it was so terrible to be purple.

Teddy closed his eyes tight to hold back his tears, but as he heard the other toys chant "Who likes purple teddy bears? Who likes purple teddy bears?" the tears came rolling down his purple cheeks

Suddenly, the toys got very quiet. Santa's helpers were getting ready to pack the sleigh for Santa's big trip. All the toys were anxiously waiting to be put in the sleigh.

As Teddy slowly opened his eyes, he noticed a door had been left open. He wanted to run away. He did not want anyone to be unhappy getting him for Christmas. He slid off the table very quietly and dropped to the floor.

Teddy picked himself up and ran out the door
as fast as his chubby little legs could carry him.

He kept on running and running and running...

...until he was so tired he could not run any farther.

By this time it was beginning to grow dark. Soft, fluffy snowflakes were falling out of the dim sky. Teddy looked up and watched them floating down. He liked the cool feeling when they landed on his face.

He tried to catch the snowflakes in his mouth and in his hands. Playing in the snow made Teddy smile, and he started to laugh and forget about his troubles.

After a while Teddy heard something. He stopped to listen.

Jingle, jingle, jingle.

He looked around, but all he could see was more snow coming down.

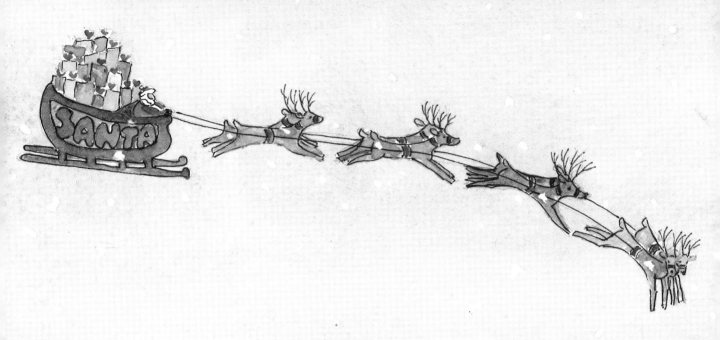

Then Teddy heard a voice say, "Ho, ho, ho!" He looked up and saw Santa, the sleigh, and Santa's reindeer all coming toward him.

"Whoa there," Santa called to his reindeer. "Whoa!"
He jumped out of the sleigh and picked up the
teddy bear. "You silly little teddy bear," Santa said
as he wiped a tear from the bear's face. "Why did
you run away?"

Trying not to cry, Teddy whispered, "Nobody will
want me because I am purple."

Santa shook his head as he climbed back into his sleigh, placing Teddy on the seat beside him. "You just wait and see," he said. He called to his reindeer, and they were on their way.

Soon the tired teddy bear was fast asleep.

When they arrived at Sam's house, Teddy was still sleeping. Santa gently put the teddy bear under the Christmas tree. Santa noticed the cookies and milk, which made him smile. "Sam remembered," he said as he sat down and enjoyed the treats. "Mmmm, that was really good."

As Santa got ready to leave, Teddy woke up and sadly looked up at him. Santa smiled and shook his head. He told Teddy, "You will like Sam, and he's going to like you too!" And then Santa was on his way.

Early Christmas morning, Sam came running down the stairs. He looked under the tree and shouted in a loud and excited voice, "A teddy bear!"

Sam picked up his teddy bear and hugged Teddy so tight that the bear squeaked.

Sam looked at his teddy bear again and said, "A purple teddy bear! How did Santa know that purple is my favorite color?" He hugged his teddy bear even tighter.

Teddy was so happy to be purple!

Janie Tesch-Cassady was born and raised in Minnesota. She attended St. Cloud State Teachers College. After college, she married and moved to Buffalo, Minnesota, where her husband practiced law. She taught first grade until the fourth of her five daughters was born. Art and writing were always a passion. She wrote *The Purple Teddy Bear* while in college. Her professor had encouraged her to publish it, but life got in the way as she became a busy mom, talented artist, and volunteer. Now a great-grandmother, she was encouraged to pursue her writing career. She currently lives in Plymouth, Minnesota. *The Purple Teddy Bear* is her first published story.